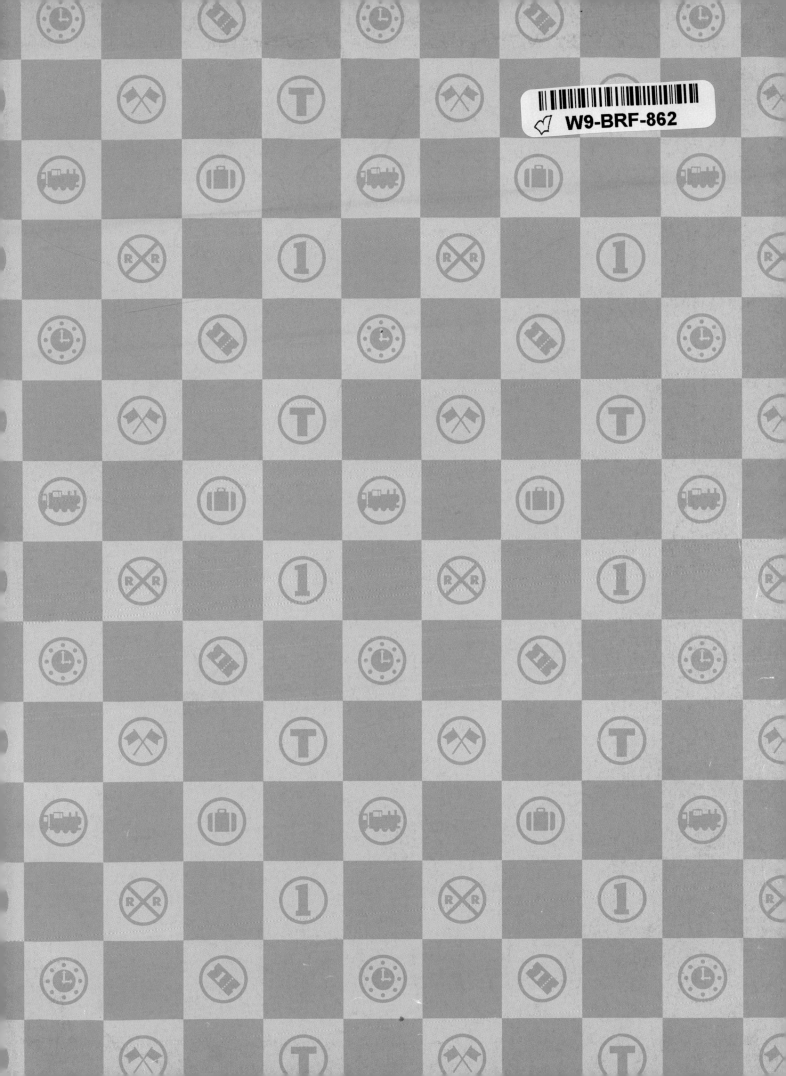

EGMONT

We bring stories to life

First published in Great Britain 2012 by Dean,
an imprint of Egmont UK Limited
239 Kensington High Street, London W8 6SA

HiT entertainment

Thomas the Tank Engine & Friends™

CREATED BY BRITT ALLCROFT
Based on the Railway Series by the Reverend W Awdry
© 2012 Gullane (Thomas) LLC. A HIT Entertainment company.
Thomas the Tank Engine & Friends and Thomas & Friends are trademarks of Gullane (Thomas) Limited.
Thomas the Tank Engine & Friends and Design is Reg. U.S. Pat. & Tm. Off.

ISBN 978 0 6035 6721 6
52805/1
Printed in Italy

THOMAS & FRIENDS™

Favourite Stories

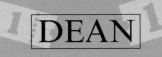
DEAN

This book belongs to

ANTHONY

Contents

Thomas, Percy and the Squeak

One summer morning, the engines were feeling very excited.

The famous singer, Alicia Botti, was coming to Sodor to sing at a concert. All of the engines wanted to collect her from the Docks.

"I will be chosen," said James. "I'm the shiniest engine."

"But I'm the most important," huffed Gordon.

"The Fat Controller might choose me," Thomas said, hopefully.

Percy pulled up next to Gordon. His face was very dirty.

"Well, one thing's for sure," snorted Gordon. "The Fat Controller certainly won't choose dirty Percy!"

The next day, The Fat Controller announced which engine would collect the singer.

But The Fat Controller didn't choose Gordon or James. He chose Thomas!

"Make sure you are squeaky clean," said The Fat Controller.

"Yes, Sir," said Thomas, proudly.

Thomas hurried off to be cleaned. He wheeshed up next to Percy. "Move over," said Thomas. "I'm the important engine today!"

"But I need a washdown!" wailed Percy. "My passengers will laugh at me!"

"You'll have to wait," Thomas huffed. "Today, I have to be squeaky clean."

"Then I'll have to go without being cleaned," said Percy, unhappily. And he chuffed away, still dirty.

Soon Thomas was shiny and clean. But as he was coupled to Annie and Clarabel, he heard a strange squeaking noise.

"What's that?" asked Thomas, anxiously.

His Driver quickly oiled Annie and Clarabel's wheels. "That should take care of the annoying squeak," he said.

Thomas headed off to collect Alicia Botti.

As he passed a lighthouse, Thomas heard the squeak again!

He was very worried. What was making that noise?

Thomas hoped it would stop before he reached the Docks.

But as Thomas arrived at the Docks, he was still squeaking!

Alicia Botti was waiting to be collected with The Fat Controller. Thomas hoped she would not notice the noise.

The Fat Controller held Clarabel's door open for Alicia Botti to climb aboard.

But as she was boarding the train, Alicia spotted a little mouse in the carriage!

"SQUEAK!" said the mouse.

"**EEEEK**! A mouse!" screamed Alicia Botti. "I can't possibly travel in coaches full of mice!"

The Fat Controller was very embarrassed and Thomas didn't feel important any more.

Just then, Percy chuffed up. He looked dirtier than ever.

"What a lovely green engine!" Alicia Botti exclaimed. "All dirty like a proper steam engine. I want him to take me to the concert."

So Alicia boarded the train and Percy steamed away. He felt very proud.

Later on, Thomas was waiting at the Washdown when Percy chuffed up beside him.

"I'm sorry I was so rude to you earlier," Thomas said. "You go first."

"Thanks, Thomas. It's good to be friends again," said Percy. "But what happened to your mouse?"

Thomas smiled. "Come with me and I'll show you," he said.

The Fat Controller had made the little mouse her very own home in the corner of the station.

And Thomas had named her Alicia!

Twin Trouble

Donald and Douglas were Scottish engines.

They were twins and they nearly always worked together.

One day, they were working very hard, pulling a heavy load through the countryside.

Further down the track, Trevor the Traction Engine was pulling a cart-load of hay.

Suddenly, one of his wheels broke and fell off on to the track!

Trevor saw Donald and Douglas approaching.

"Oh no!" cried Trevor. He knew there would be an accident.

Donald saw the cart wheel and tried to brake in time. "Stop!" Trevor cried, but it was too late.

Donald crashed off the tracks and was covered in hay.

"You need a haircut!" laughed Douglas.

Donald didn't think it was very funny, but he laughed when the wind blew the hay on to Douglas! Now Douglas was cross, too.

Before long, the twins were hardly speaking to one another.

The next day, The Fat Controller wanted an engine to help Duck at the power plant. "May I go, Sir?" asked Donald.

"I'm afraid I only need one engine," said The Fat Controller.

"I am one engine," said Donald. "I don't want to work with Douglas." The Fat Controller was surprised, but he agreed.

Thomas was worried. "Won't you miss each other?" he asked.

"No," said Douglas. "I'll work much better on my own."

"I'm off!" said Donald, racing off to the power plant.

Donald enjoyed working with Duck and taking coal trucks along the coastal track. But soon things started to go wrong.

"Did you shunt those trucks on to the other line?" asked Donald.

"You said you wanted them on the other line," Duck replied.

"I didn't mean that line, I meant the other line," said Donald.

"Douglas would have known what I meant," he added.

Meanwhile, Douglas was working on his own.

Douglas thought the Island of Sodor looked beautiful, but he was sad because he had no one to share it with.

Although he tried hard not to, Douglas was beginning to miss his twin. He decided that he would speak to Donald that night.

"Have you come to say you are sorry?" said Donald.

This made Douglas very cross. "I've nothing to be sorry for!" he said, steaming away in a huff.

The next day, Donald was in a bad mood. He wasn't looking at what he was doing.

Duck saw that he was too close to the buffers.
"Whoa!" Duck said.

But Donald thought Duck had said 'Go,' so he rolled back and crashed into the buffers.

Duck was shocked. "What were you thinking?" he said.

"This would never have happened if you were working with Douglas," said Donald's Driver, crossly.

Duck couldn't pull Donald back on to the rails, so he went to get some help.

"Donald's in trouble!" Duck said to Douglas.

"Oh, no!" cried Douglas. "I'm on my way!"

And he steamed out of the depot as fast as he could.

Douglas gently pulled Donald back on to the track.

"Thank you," said Donald. "And I'm really sorry!"

"Yes, I'm sorry, too!" said Douglas.

"Good! I'm glad you're friends again!" said Duck.

From then on, Donald and Douglas always worked well together and they never argued – well, hardly ever!

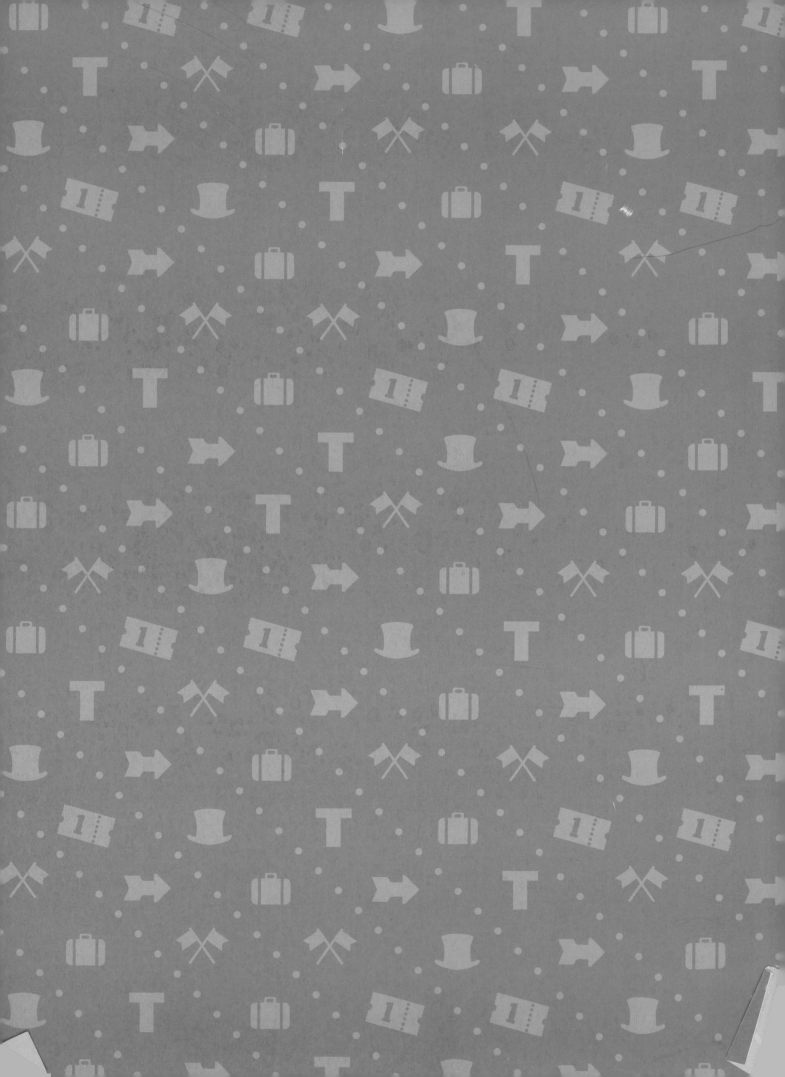

Thomas, James and the
Red Balloon

One day, The Fat Controller sent Thomas to take something very important to the Airfield.

"What have you got there?" asked Percy.

"It's a balloon," said Thomas. "A very special balloon."

And he chuffed away, leaving Percy feeling very curious.

Thomas arrived at the Airfield.

Hot air was pumped into the balloon, and people were climbing into the big basket underneath.

Then, as if by magic, the balloon rose silently into the sky.

Everyone was very impressed!

Just then, James arrived with some coaches.
"What is that?" James asked, when he saw the balloon.

"It's a hot air balloon," explained Thomas.
"Holidaymakers can ride in it."

"But what if it takes our passengers away?" said James.

"I hadn't thought of that!" replied Thomas. He felt worried.

The balloon floated high in the sky, taking people on trips all over the Island of Sodor. James did not like it.

"Passengers belong on trains," said James, crossly. "Not in silly balloons!"

After that, wherever James went on the Island, he saw the red balloon.

And Thomas and James often had to take passengers to the Airfield, so they could go for a ride in the balloon.

One day, Thomas and James were waiting at a level crossing for Bertie to cross the line.

Suddenly, the balloon came drifting towards them!

"Help!" cried the balloon Driver. "We're out of hot air!"

CRASH! BANG! WALLOP! The balloon landed on top of James! He was so scared, he let out a huge burst of steam. **WHOOSH!** The balloon rose up into the air again.

"Well done, James!" said his Driver. "Your hot air did the trick!"

"Oh no!" cried Thomas. "You saved it!" James was not pleased.

Later on, James arrived at the station. The Fat Controller was waiting on the platform. He was very pleased with James.

"But I wish it hadn't helped!" said James. "Now our passengers will all ride in the balloon instead."

"Don't worry!" The Fat Controller laughed. "The holidaymakers will all need a lift to and from the Airfield by train!"

James was delighted. He whistled happily and went to tell Thomas the good news.

And The Fat Controller was right. The engines were busier than ever, taking passengers to and from the Airfield.

Thomas and Bertie often had races to see who could get to the Airfield first.

All the engines started looking out for the balloon.

One day, Henry spotted it floating above him by the beach.

And Donald and Douglas liked to watch the balloon float over the engine sheds.

Now, whenever James sees the balloon, he whistles and toots loudly at it.

And sometimes, when James is asleep at night, he has pleasant dreams . . .

. . . of the red balloon floating in the sky!

It was a very exciting day at the Docks. A new engine had arrived on the Island of Sodor!

Cranky the Crane unloaded him on to the track. He was very heavy. "This makes my chin ache," said Cranky, crossly.

The Fat Controller introduced the new engine to everyone.

"This is Harvey, a crane engine," said The Fat Controller.

He had brought with him the Gentlemen from the Railway Board.

They were going to watch Harvey do a demonstration, to decide if he could join the Railway.

"What's a 'dimmer station'?" asked Percy.

"Demonstration!" said Thomas. "It's when you show off what you can do."

"Like when Thomas and I have a race," said Bertie. "Vrooooomm! Vrooooomm!"

That evening in the engine sheds, Harvey overheard the other engines talking about him.

"Harvey's different," peeped Henry.

"He doesn't even look like an engine!" said Gordon.

Poor Harvey! No one wanted to be his friend.

Thomas felt sorry for Harvey.

"Don't worry, Harvey," Thomas whispered to him.
"It takes time to make new friends!"

But Harvey wasn't sure he wanted to stay where
no one wanted him.

The next morning, Harvey spoke to The Fat Controller. "The engines don't like me, Sir," he said. "I'm too different."

"Nonsense! Being different is what makes you special," said The Fat Controller.

Harvey felt much better after that.

The Fat Controller had asked Bertie to take the Gentlemen from the Railway Board on a tour of the Island of Sodor.

Bertie was proud to be carrying such important passengers.

Out on the branch line, Percy was having trouble with his trucks. "Faster we go. Faster we go!" they cried.

"Help!" whistled Percy, as he tried to slow down.

His Driver applied the brakes, but it was too late.

CRASH! Percy came off the track and his trucks fell on to the road, right in front of Bertie. The road was blocked!

When The Fat Controller heard about the crash, he went to see Harvey. "I need you to rescue Percy and some trucks," The Fat Controller said.

"I'll do my best, Sir," said Harvey.

Harvey worked very hard. And before long, he had lifted Percy and the trucks back on to the track.

"Thank you so much," said Percy to Harvey. "I can see now that you are a Really Useful Engine. I can't wait to tell the other engines about how you rescued me!"

The Gentlemen from the Railway Board were impressed.

"That was the best demonstration of all!" The Fat Controller said. "The Gentlemen have decided that you can join the Railway."

"Thank you, Sir," said Harvey, proudly.

That evening in the sheds, the engines were talking about Harvey again. But this time it was different.

"Isn't Harvey clever!" chuffed Gordon.

"Welcome to the Sodor Railway!" the other engines called.

Harvey smiled happily. It was good to have friends.

Goodbye!

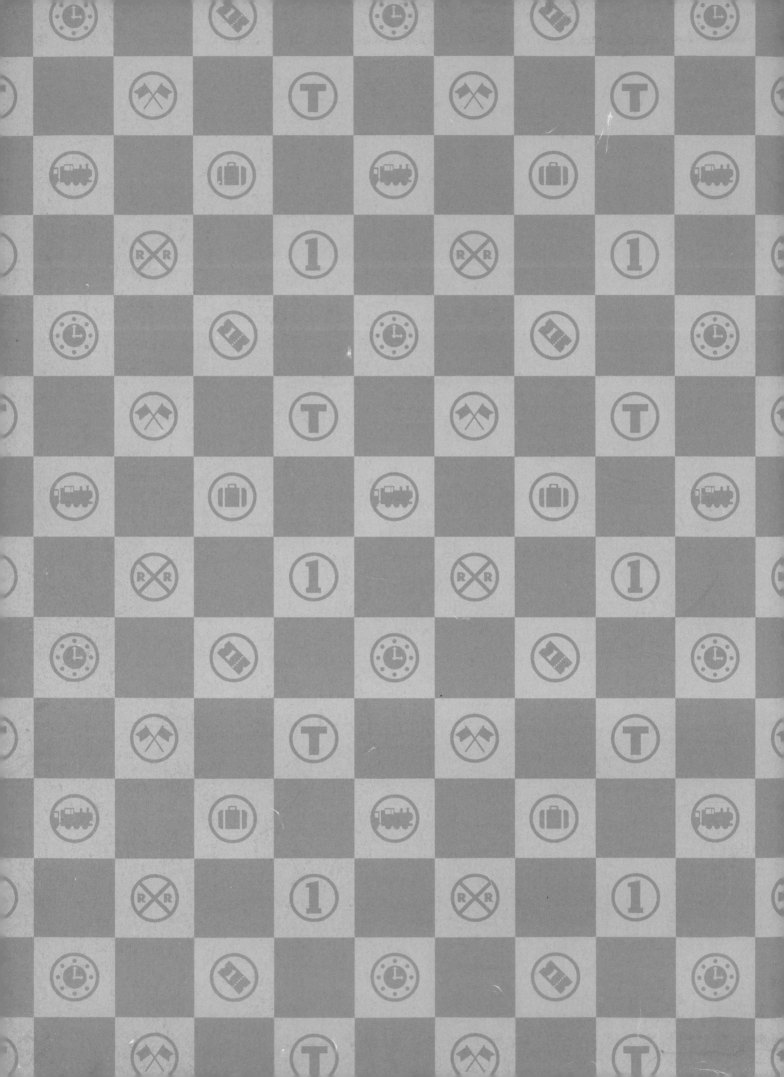